James Williams

Briefless Ballads and Legal Lyrics

second series

James Williams

Briefless Ballads and Legal Lyrics
second series

ISBN/EAN: 9783744769051

Printed in Europe, USA, Canada, Australia, Japan

Cover: Foto ©Andreas Hilbeck / pixelio.de

More available books at **www.hansebooks.com**

BRIEFLESS BALLADS

BRIEFLESS BALLADS

AND

LEGAL LYRICS

SECOND SERIES

By JAMES WILLIAMS

"You will think a lawyer has as little business with
poetry as he has with justice. Perhaps so. I have been
too partial to both."
—THOMAS LOVE PEACOCK, in *Melincourt*

LONDON
ADAM AND CHARLES BLACK
1895

CONTENTS

———◆———

(The First Series was published anonymously in 1881, and is now out
of print. Some of the following pieces have already appeared
in periodicals.)

5

Contents

Interioris amat Templi jam Pegasus aulas

Pieria in Medio plenior unda ruit.

7

Justinian at Windermere

WE took a hundredweight of books
  To Windermere between us,
Our dons had blessed our studious looks,
  Had they by chance but seen us.

Maine, Blackstone, Sandars, all were there,
  And Hallam's *Middle Ages*,
And Austin with his style so rare,
  And Poste's enticing pages.

We started well: the little inn
  Was deadly dull and quiet,
As dull as Mrs. Wood's *East Lynne*,
  Or as the verse of Wyatt.

Without distraction thus we read
   From nine until eleven,
Then rowed and sailed until we **fed**
   On potted char at seven.

Two hours of work! We could devote
   Next day to recreation,
Much illness springs, so doctors note,
   From lack of relaxation.

Let him read law on summer days,
   Who has a soul that grovels;
Better one tale of Thackeray's
   Than all Justinian's novels.

At noon we went upon the lake,
   We could not stand the slowness
Of our lone inn, so dined on steak
   (They *called* it steak) at Bowness.

Legal Lyrics

We wrestled with the steak, when lo!
    Rose Jack in such a hurry,
He saw a girl he used to know
    In Suffolk or in Surrey.

What matter which? to think that she
    Should lure him from his duty!
For Jack, I knew, would always be
    A very slave to beauty.

And so it proved, alas! for Jack
    Grew taciturn and thinner,
Was out all day alone, and back
    Too often late for dinner.

What could I do?   His walks and rows
    All led to one conclusion;
I could not read; our work, heaven knows,
    Was nothing but confusion.

Like Jack I went about alone,
  Saw Wordsworth's writing-table,
And made the higher by a stone
  The "man" upon Great Gable.

At last there came a sudden pause
  To all his wanderings *solus*,
He learned what writers on the laws
  Of Rome had meant by *dolus*.

The Suffolk (was it Surrey ?) flirt
  Without a pang threw over
Poor Jack and all his works like dirt,
  And caught a richer lover.

We read one morning more to say
  We had not been quite idle,
And then to end the arduous day
  Enjoyed a swim in Rydal.

Next day the hundredweight of books
  Was packed once more in cases,
We left the lakes and hills and brooks
  And southward turned our faces.

Three months, and then the Oxford Schools;
  Our unbelieving college
Saw better than ourselves what fools
  Pretend sometimes to knowledge.

Curst questions! Jack did only one,
  He gave as his opinion
That of the Roman jurists none
  Had lived before Justinian.

I answered two, but all I did
  Was lacking in discretion,
I reckoned guardianship amid
  The *vitia* of possession.

13

My second shot was wider still,

    I held that *commodata*

Could not attest a prætor's will

    Because of *culpa lata*.

We waited fruitlessly that night,

    There came no blue *testamur*,*

Nor was Jack's heavy heart made light

    By that sweet word *Amamur*.

* Since the above was written, the *testamur*, like many other institutions dear to the old order of Oxford men, has been superseded.

A Vision of Legal Shadows

A CASE at chambers left for my opinion
  Had taxed my brain until the noon of night,
I read old law, and loathed the long dominion
      Of fiction over right.

I had consulted Coke and Cruise and Chitty,
  The works where ancient learning reigns supreme,
Until exhausted nature, moved with pity,
      Sent me a bookman's dream.

Six figures, all gigantic as Gargantua,
  Floated before my eyes, and all the six
Were shades like those that once the bard of Mantua
      Saw by the shore of Styx.

The first was one with countenance imperious,

His toga dim with centuries of dust ;

" My name," quoth he, " is Aulus and Agerius,*

My voice is hoarse with rust.

" Yet once I played my part in law proceedings,

And writers wrote of one they never saw,

I gave their point to formulæ and pleadings,

I lived but in the law."

The second had a countenance perfidious ;

What wonder ?   Prætors launched their formulæ

In vain against Numerius Negidius,

And not a whit cared he.

---

* Aulus Agerius and Numerius Negidius are names continually
occurring in the Roman institutional writers as typical names of
parties to legal process, corresponding very much to the John Stiles
and John Nokes of the older English law-books, and the Amr and
Zaid of Mohammedan law.   John Stiles was frequently contracted
to J. S.

Legal Lyrics

With voice of high contempt he greeted Aulus;
  " In interdicts thou wast mine enemy,
Once passed no day that students did not call us
    As parties, me and thee.

" On paper I was plaintiff or defendant,
  On paper thou wast evermore the same;
We lived apart, a life that was transcendant,
    For it was but a name.

" I hate thee, Aulus, hate thee," low he muttered,
  " It was by thee that I was always tricked,
My unsubstantial bread I ate unbuttered
    In dread of interdict.

" And yet 'twas but the sentiment I hated :
  Like thee I ne'er was drunk e'en *vi* or *clam*,†

† *Vi* and *clam* were part of the form of the interdict, which was a mode of procedure by which the prætor settled the right of possession of landed property.

With wine that was no wine my thirst was sated.

Like thee I was a sham."

Two country hinds in 'broidered smocks next

followed,

Each trundled him a cart-wheel by the spokes,

Oblivion now their names hath well-nigh swallowed,

For they were Stiles and Nokes.

They spake no word, for speech to them was

grievous,

With bovine eyes they supplicated me;

" We wot not what ye will, but prithee leave us,

Unlettered folk are we."

" Go," said I, " simple ones, and break your fallows,

Crush autumn apples in the cider press,

Law, gaffer Stiles, thy humble name still hallows,

Contracted to J. S."

Another pair of later time succeeded,

   With buckles on their shoes and silken hose,

A garb that told it was to them who heeded

       John Doe's and Richard Roe's.

" Ah me ! I was a casual ejector,*

   In the brave days of old," I heard one say ;

" I knew Elizabeth, the Lord Protector

       I spake with yesterday."

To whom in contradiction snarled the other,

   " There was no living blood our veins to fill.

Both you and I were nought but shadows, brother,

       And we are shadows still."

Room for a lady, room, as at Megiddo

   The hosts made way for passage of the king,

* The casual ejector was John Doe, who was, like Richard Roe, an entirely imaginary person, of much importance in the old action of ejectment abolished in 1852.

   (2)   19

For from the darkness crept there forth a widow
    In weeds and wedding ring.

"I am the widow, I, whereof the singers

    Of Scotland sang, their **cruel** words **so smote**

My tender heart, that ofttimes itched my fingers

    To take them by the throat.

"**He scoffed** at me, dour bachelor of Glasgow, ‡

    If I existed not for him, the knave,

'Twas all his fault who let some bonnie lass go

    Unwedded to her grave."

‡ The allusion is to the " Advocates' Widows Fund," subscribed to by all members of the Scottish bar, married or unmarried. The non-**existent** widow of the unmarried advocate has been a frequent subject of legal verse. See "**The Bachelor's** Dream," by John Rankine, (*Journal of Jurisprudence*, vol. xxii. p. 155), " My Widow," by David Crichton (*id.* vol. xxiv. p. 51).

The Squire's Daughter

WE crawled about the nursery
  In tenderest years in tether,
At six we waded in the sea
  And caught our colds together.

At ten we practised playing at
  A kind of heathen cricket,
A croquet mallet was the bat,
  The Squire's old hat the wicket.

At twelve, the cricket waxing slow,
  With home-made bow and arrow
We took to shooting—once I know
  I all but hit a sparrow.

She took birds' nests from easy trees,

    I climbed the oaks and ashes,

'Twas deadly work **for hands and knees,**

    Deplorable for sashes.

At hide and seek one summer day

    We played in merry laughter,

'Twas then she hid her heart away,

    I never found it after.

So time slipped by until my call,

    For out of the professions

I chose the Bar as best of all,

    And joined the Loamshire Sessions.

The reason for it was that there

    Her father, short and pursy,

Doled out scant justice in the chair

    And even scanter mercy.

As Holofernes lost his head
  To Judith of Bethulia,
So I fell victim, but instead
  Of Judith it was Julia.

My speech left juries in the dark,
  Of Julia I was thinking,
And once I heard a coarse remark
  About a fellow drinking.

I practised verse in leisure time
  Both in and out of season,
It was indubitably rhyme,
  Occasionally reason.

I lacked the cheek to tell my woes,
  Had not concealment fed on
My damask cheek, but left my nose
  With twice its share of red on?

Too horrible was this suspense,
    At last, in desperation
I went to Loamshire on pretence
    Of death of a relation.

The Squire was beaming ; " Julia's gone
    To London for a visit,
But with a wedding coming on
    That's not surprising, is it ?

Old friends like you will think, no doubt,
    That she is young to marry,
But ever since she first came out,
    She's been engaged to Harry."

Her Letter in Chambers

I SAT by the fire and watched it blaze,
  And dreamed that she wrote me a letter,
And for that dream to the end of my days
  To Fancy I owe myself debtor.

Next day there came the postman's knock,
  The morning was bright and sunny,
And showed me a sheaf of circulars, stock
  Attempts to get hold of my money.

'Mid correspondence of this dull kind
  A dainty notelet lay hidden,
It seemed as though it had half a mind
  To consider itself forbidden.

The writing was like herself, complete,
  With a touch of her queenly bearing,
So Venus wrote when she ordered in Crete
  Her doves to take her an airing.

Briefless Ballads, etc.

Inside it was just as promising,
  'Twas a pressing invitation
To dine at her house to-morrow, and bring
  My book for her approbation.

For I have published, be it confessed,
  A little volume of verses,
And in the volume whatever is best
  The praise of herself rehearses.

I sit by the fire, and again I dream
  A happier dream than ever,
I see her beautiful eyes soft gleam
  As she murmurs, " How lovely—how clever !"

Her criticism may be commonplace,
  But who can be angry after
Now sweet with pity he marks her face,
  Now bright with impulsive laughter?

Law and Poetry

In days of old did law and rime
    A common pathway follow,
For Themis in the mythic time
    Was sister of Apollo.

The Hindu statutes tripped in feet
    As daintily as Dryads,
And law in Wales to be complete
    Was versified in triads.

The wise Alfonso of Castile
    Composed his code in metre
Thereby to make its flavour feel
    A little bit the sweeter.

But law and rime were found to be
    A trifle inconsistent,
And now in statutes poetry
    Is wholly non-existent.

Still here and there some advocate
  Before his fellows know it
Has had bestowed on him by fate
  The laurel of the poet.

Let him who has been honoured so,
  In truth a *rara avis*,
Find precedents in Cicero
  And our Chief Justice Davis;

And more than all in Cino; he,
  So plaintive a narrator
Of fair Selvaggia's cruelty,
  Won fame as a glossator.

Let him remember Thomas More
  And Scott and Alciatus,
And Grotius with an ample store
  Of most divine afflatus.

28

But let him, if his bread and cheese
  Depend on his profession,
Bethink him that the art of these
  Was not their sole possession.

The stream that flows from Helicon
  Is scarcely a Pactolus,
A richer prize is theirs who con
  Dull treatises on *dolus*.

'Tis well that some bold spirits dare
  To cut themselves asunder
From bonds of law like old Molière,
  While lawyers gaze in wonder.

The world had been a poorer place
  Had Goethe lived by pleading
Or Tasso won a hopeless case
  With Ariosto leading.

Somewhere

SOMEWHERE in **a** distant star,

Cities of Cocaigne there are,

Paradises of the Bar.

Somewhere 'neath another sun

Counsel cease to see **the** fun

Lurking in a judge's **pun.**

Somewhere courts are fair to see,

Beauty joins utility,

Ushers answer courteously.

Somewhere there are bailiwicks

Which for dock defences fix

Nothing under three-five-six.

Briefless Ballads, etc.

Somewhere rises struggle sore

For revisorships no more,

Every shire has half a score.

Somewhere educated thought

Scientifically taught

Cross-examines as it ought.

Somewhere judgments are obeyed,

Executions are not stayed,

Fees are almost always paid.

Somewhere County Councils press

Banquets on the circuit mess,

Fleshpots in the wilderness.

Somewhere at Assizes grow

Prosecutions row on row,

Every man has six or so.

Somewhere, eager but for right,

Court and counsel cease to cite

Pointless cases recondite.

Somewhere headnotes give the ground

Whereupon the judges found

Judgments generally sound.

Somewhere juries use their sense,

Basing on the evidence

Verdicts of intelligence.

Somewhere rich embroideries

Woven cunningly of lies

Part in twain at truth's clear eyes.

Somewhere justice grows from wrong,

Till the right that suffered long

Sings at last its triumph song.

Legal Lyrics

Somewhere—even in a place
Peopled by a perfect race—
One side holds a losing case.

Somewhere since the world began
Heaven hath made an honest man,
Somewhere in Aldebaran.

Roman Law

I AM a "coach" in Roman law by fate,
  But Nature must have meant me for a poet,
And while I struggle with a rule or date,
  Poetic thoughts intrude before I know it.

The changing sunshine on the summer sea
  Drives forth the law of *cessio bonorum*,
Peculium castrense speaks to me
  Of Horace and his *Dulce et decorum*.

I see the matine bee among the flowers
  Instead of *testamentum militare*,
And wander far away from agent's powers
  To picture me again some Maud or Mary.

In truth there is no sequence in the thought,
  Why should the title *De Societate*
Suggest, not trading partners, as it ought,
  But visions of my last night's valse with Katie?

34

But worse than this, when I have done my task,
   Stern law again asserts her domination,
'Tis cruel 'mid the new-mown hay to bask,
   And find one's mind is running on novation ;

Or in the dusk, when glow-worms light the moss,
   To hear the distant voice of Philomela
Expound the three varieties of *dos*
   And wax right eloquent about *tutela*.

I had a little respite yesterday,
   Dining with one who well knew how to dine us,
But when I slept, the charm soon fled away,
   I dreamed I was a *prætor peregrinus*.

Dismasted in the deep of law I lie,
   A poor reward it is to stand confessed as
The Virgil of the interdict *de vi*,
   The Petrarch of the *patria potestas*.

(3)   35

Bologna

I GO from colonnade to colonnade

In streets that Dante trod, and past the towers

Aslant toward heaven, and listen to the hours

Chimed by the bells of choirs where Dante prayed.

They cease ; then lo ! the foot of time seems stayed

Five hundred years and more, I find me bowers

Where sweet and noble ladies weave them flowers

For one who reads Boccaccio in the shade.

The cowlèd students halt by two and threes

To hear the voice come thrilling through the trees,

Then tear themselves away to themes more trite.

Anon I mark the diligent hands that turn

Unlovely parchment scrolls whereby to learn

The beauty of inexorable right.

A Garden Party in the Temple

On hospitable thoughts intent
To me the Inner Temple sent
    An invitation,
A garden party 'twas to be,
And I accepted readily
    And with elation;
Good reason too, but oft the seeds
Of reason flower in senseless deeds.

I stood as savage as a bear,
For not a human being there
    Knew I from Adam

I heard around in various tones,

" *So* glad to see you, Mr. Jones ; "

   " Good morning, Madam."

It seemed so painfully absurd

To stand and never speak a word.

I brought my doom upon myself,

And there I was upon the shelf

   In melancholy.

Why, say you, did I go at all ?

I once met Chloris at a ball,

   And in my folly

I went and suffered all this pain

In hopes to see her once again.

Of strawberries a pound at least

I ate, and made myself a beast

   With tea and sherry ;

Legal Lyrics

And raspberries I ate and trembled,
Until I felt that I resembled
    Myself a berry,
But 'twas the berry that at school
We used to call a gooseberry fool.

The I. C. R. V.* band droned on,
While guests had come and guests had gone
    Since my arrival ;
My brow grew gloomier with despair,
And on it sat the guilty air
    Of a survival
Of some remorse for ancient crimes
Wrought in the pre-historic times.

My seventh cup of tea was done,
My seventh glass of wine begun,
    Then of her coming

* Inns of Court Rifle Volunteers.

39

Briefless Ballads, etc.

I was aware, nor shall forget
How she and that brown sherry set
  My brains a-humming ;
Well should I be rewarded soon
For all the weary afternoon.

Her eyes looked vaguely into mine
Without as much as half a sign
  Of recognition.
My heart, my heart ! the blow was sore,
But you have often been before
  In this condition ;
As said the bard of old, those eyes
Are not my only Paradise.†

    † Dante, Par. xviii. 21.

The Spinning-House of the Future

" Cada puta hile."—*Don Quixote*, i. 46.

WITHOUT my dinner here I lie,

    And all because that proctor

With her stout bull-dogs passed, and I

    Mocked her.

For Clara is at Girton too,

    That dragon is her tutor,

I threatened once what I would do,

    Shoot her.

Her life by Clara's tears was saved,

    Wherefore she doth detest me,

And hither hungry and unshaved

    Pressed me.

I would that I could have commenced

    An action 'gainst that devil,

Like that once brought by Kemp against

Neville.*

To her I owe the statute framed

That one against it sinning

Should dwell within the house that's named

Spinning.

Ah me ! it runs in sections three :

Who speaks to Girton student

Is fined to teach him how to be

Prudent.

Who loves a Girton girl must do

Twelve months on bread and water,

From a digestive point of view

Slaughter.

---

* An action brought in 1861 by a dressmaker at Cambridge against the Vice-Chancellor for false imprisonment in the Spinning-House (the University prison). The Court of Common Pleas held *inter alia* that no action lies against a judge for a judicial decision on a matter within his jurisdiction (10 Common Bench Reports, New Series, 523).

Legal Lyrics

Who kisses her commits a crime
    By hanging expiated,
And she in tears must spend her time
    Gated.

Would that at Oxford I had been,
    At Balliol or at Merton,
And then I never should have seen
    Girton.

Go down I must, no more shall I
    And Clara cross the same bridge;
Still, Granta, art thou her and my
    Cambridge.

Some day on this her eyes may light,
    This doggerel stiff and jointless,
And she may own it is not quite
    Pointless.

How we Found our Verdict

WE sat in the jury-box, twelve were we all,
And the clock was just pointing to ten in the hall,
His Lordship he bowed to the jury, and we
Bowed back to his Lordship as gravely as he.

The case of *De Weller v. Jones* was the first,
And we all settled down and prepared for the worst
When old Smithers, Q.C., began slowly to preach
Of a promise of marriage and action for breach.

A barmaid the plaintiff was, wondrous the skill
Wherewith she was wont her tall tankards to fill,
The defendant, a publican, sought for his bride
Such a paragon, urged by professional pride.

44

But the course of true love ran no smoother for her
Than the Pas de Calais or the bark of a fir,
The defendant discovered a widow with gold
In the bank and the plaintiff was left in the cold.

An hour Smithers spoke, and he said that the heart
Of the plaintiff at Jones's fell touch flew apart,
But a cheque for a thousand might help to repair
The destruction effected by love and despair.

Miss de Weller was called, and in ladylike tones
She described all the injury suffered from Jones,
How he called her at first " Angelina," and this
Soon cooled to " Miss Weller," and lastly to " Miss."

But the jury were shaken a little when Gore
Cross-examined about her engagements before,
For Jones was the sixth of the strings to her bow
And with five other verdicts she solaced her woe.

Re-examined by Smithers, she won us again,

For the tears of a maid are a terror to men,

Then his Lordship awoke from his nap and explained

How love that is frequent is love that is feigned.

Miss de Weller looked daggers, and under the paint

Of her cheeks she grew pale and fell down in a faint,

She played her trump-card in the late afternoon,

For damages satisfy girls who can swoon.

Till she fainted most thought that a farthing would do,

Though I was in favour of pounds—one or two ;

But after the faint—and she *was* so well dressed—

At a hundred the void in her heart was assessed.

A Greek Libel

ARCHILOCHUS.

NEOBULE, yesternight
Saw I thee in beauty dight,
On thy head a myrtle spray
Cast its shadow as the day
By the stars was put to flight.

Twining on thy temples white
Roses gave the myrtle light,
Sign thou wilt not say me nay,
        Neobule.

Loosened from its coilèd height
Streamed thy hair in thy despite
On thy shoulders soft to stray
And to bid the bard essay
Never but of thee to write,
        Neobule.

47

NEOBULE.

Sorry poet, who dost dare

Cast bold glances on my hair,

Let thy most presumptuous eyes

Seek another enterprise,

Ceasing now **to** linger **there.**

Hearken, I can tell thee where

Grow the bushes that will spare

Rods to teach thee humbler guise.

Sorry poet.

Know I not that **I am fair?**

Need thy halting verse declare

What **my mirror** daily cries?

Rid me **of thy** silly sighs,

Rid me of thy hateful stare,

Sorry poet.

Legal Lyrics

ARCHILOCHUS.

Neobule, poets see
Dreams of things that are to be.
Vengeance is the poet's trade,
Come, iambus, to my aid
'Gainst the fools who scoff at me.
All the world will laugh with glee
When they mark my verses free
Grasp thee like a pillory.
And thy scorn with scorn repaid,
　　　Neobule.

E'en in death thou canst not flee
From the doom the Fates decree.
When my satire's keenest blade
Cuts thee to the heart, fond maid,
I shall laugh, but what of thee,
　　　Neobule?

Le Temps Passé

THOSE brave old days when King Abuse did reign

We sigh for, but we shall not see again.

Then Eldon sowed the seed of equity

That grew to bounteous harvest, and with glee

A Bar of modest numbers shared the grain.

Then lived the pleaders who could issues feign,

Who blushed not to aver that France or Spain

Was in the Ward of Chepe ;* no more can be

                Those brave old days.

* See, for instance, the well-known case of *Mostyn* v. *Fabrigas*, in which the plaintiff declared that the defendant on the 1st of September, in the year 1771, made an assault upon the said plaintiff at Minorca, to wit, at London, in the parish of St. Mary-le-bow, in the Ward of Cheap.

Briefless Ballads, etc.

O'er pauper settlements men fought amain,

And golden guineas followed in their train,

John Doe then flourished like a lusty tree,

And Richard Roe brought many a noble fee,

We mourn in unremunerated pain

         Those brave old days.

Lawn Tennis in the Temple Gardens

NOT in contempt but to our sport inclined
Smile on us, shades of Judges short and tall
Portrayed on windows of the Temple Hall;
There was a time that ye grave thoughts resigned,
Then, warm with sack, the Serjeants' hearts waxed
    kind,
In mirth Lords Keepers danced the galliard all,
        Not in contempt.

Of pleasures past the shadows here we find,
Gay strife on brighter swards we thus recall,
Where maiden laughter winged the flying ball;
Declare us, fair ones, with a merry mind
        Not in contempt.

A Ballade of Lost Law

(Spirit of Lord Eldon speaks)

THIS England is gone staring mad,

She hath abolished Chancery,*

See the long lines of suitors, sad

To find themselves unwontedly

After one day of trial free.

Pleading and seals have gone their way.

" I know," said I, "that after me

Too quickly comes the evil day."

---

* The Court of Chancery was merged in the High Court of Justice
in 1875.

(Spirit of Lord Lyndhurst speaks

I was Chief Baron, and I had

A Court of Law and Equity,†

The Courts at Westminster were clad

With ancient glory fair to see.

Now County Courts have come to be

Exalted high on our decay,

And every whit as good as we;

Too quickly comes the evil day.

(Shade of Butler speaks)

In days of yore we used to pad

Our deeds with words of **certainty**;

Alas! **that** now the office lad

Is qualified to grant in **fee!**

---

† In the days of Lord Lyndhurst the old Court of Exchequer had
equitable as well as common law jurisdiction.

Lost is our old supremacy,

Lost is the delicate display

Of learning on *pur autre vie*;

Too quickly comes the evil day.

L'ENVOI

(The Three in Chorus)

Thurlow, to thee we bend the knee,

When law was law, then men were gay,

'Tis down with port and up with téa,

Too quickly comes the evil day.

Comœdia Juris

Est omne jus forense quasi comœdia ;

Hic advocatus maximas partes agit

Laudatus undique a procuratoribus,

Labore vocis redditus ditissimus ;

Cui brevia nil forensis et quaestus valent

Silenter ille spectat, at pro præmio

Fruitur quietus optime comœdia.

Cases

Cases

MYLWARD v. WELDON

[The plaintiff was committed to the Fleet Prison on Feb. 8, 1596,
by order of the Lord Keeper, for drawing a replication of six-score
sheets containing much impertinent matter which might well have
been contained in sixteen. On Feb. 10 the Lord Keeper ordered
that on the following Saturday the Warden of the Fleet should
cut a hole through the replication, and put the plaintiff's head
through the hole and let it hang about his shoulders with the
written side outwards, and lead the plaintiff bareheaded and
barefaced round about Westminster Hall, and show him at the
bar of all the courts, and so back to the Fleet.—Abridged from
Spence's *Equitable Jurisdiction*, vol. i. p. 376.]

'GAINST Weldon Mylward files a bill,

But doth his replication fill

With scandalous and idle matter,

That would disgrace the maddest hatter.

　　　　　　Woe is me for Mylward !

59

'Twas sixscore sheets, it might have been

Contained, and amply, in sixteen ;

So after that the court hath risen

Must Mylward Fleetward go to prison.

      Woe is me for Mylward !

And two days afterwards 'tis meet

That by the Warden of the Fleet

He be led on in slow progression

Through every court that sits in session.

      Woe is me for Mylward !

The pleading writ with words so fair

Must Mylward like a tabard wear,

A hole therein, the Warden cuts it,

A head put through it, Mylward puts it.

      Woe is me for Mylward !

The bar makes merry at his shame;

What careth he?   He winneth fame,

Three hundred years his reputation

Hath rested on that replication.

           Woe is me for Mylward!

HAMPDEN *v.* WALSH

(1 Queen's Bench Division, 189)

" FIVE hundred pounds as stake I'll lay,"

Says Hampden, "that by such a day

No man of science proves to me

That earth not flat but round must be;

The earth is flat, and flats are they."

The sum Walsh holds right willingly;

But Wallace by philosophy

Proves roundness, and would take away

        Five hundred pounds.

"Proof me no proofs," quoth Hampden, "Nay,

Let Wallace get it if he may,

I'll sue Walsh for it." So sues he.

"Let Wallace," hold the judges three,

"Take nought, let Walsh to Hampden **pay**

Five **hundred pounds.**"

WILLIS *v.* THE BISHOP OF OXFORD

(2 Probate Division, 192)

AID me, **Muses!** my endeavour is to **sing a woful**
song,

How a very learned bishop in the Arches Court went
wrong.

Aid me, for *duplex querela* is an uninviting theme,

And the practice of the Arches raises no poetic
dream.

'Tis the Reverend Child Willis, child in name but not
in age,

Comes he to the Court of Arches burning with a
noble rage,

Filing his *duplex querela*, claiming for himself thereby

Vicarage of Drayton Parslow, or to know the reason
why.

" Reason why?" the bishop answers; "that is not so
far to seek.

Little Latin have you, Willis, innocent are you of
Greek.

You were specially examined by my good Archdeacon Pott ;

He reported to me promptly, ' Greek and Latin all
forgot,

Non idoneus is Willis, *minus et sufficiens,*

He may have a *sanum corpus*, but he lacks a *sana
mens.*'"

"Nay," says Willis, "such an answer is but trifling
  with the court,
I have preached a Latin sermon, and the classics are
  my forte,
You must name the books I failed in, you must give
  me every chance
Of a fresh examination at the hands of Lord Penzance."
Lord Penzance supported Willis: "Bishop, you must
  file," **said he,**
"Some more tangible objection, some less vague and
  general plea.
As it stands I cannot gather what it is you ploughed
  him **in,**
Whether Hellenistic aorists or the Latin word for sin."
But alas! the **world** has never **known** as yet what
  Willis **did,**
In the breast of the Archdeacon still **it** lies a secret
  hid.

Legal Lyrics

Was his Latin prose defective? Did his style of
  writing show

More resemblance to Tertullian than to Tullius
  Cicero?

Were his dates a little shaky? Could it, could it be
  that he

Confidently made Augustine flourish at a date B.C.?

None will know save Pott, Archdeacon, for alas! the
  patroness

Showed no mercy to Child Willis in the day of his
  distress.

She revoked the presentation, leaving Willis in the lurch,

One of undisputed learning preached in Drayton
  Parslow church.

Doubly barren was his triumph, it was not a twelve-
  month ere

Death set up *his* Court of Arches, Willis did not
  triumph there.

65

DASHWOOD v. JERMYN

(12 Chancery Division, 776)

CAPTAIN DASHWOOD, who had been
In the service of the Queen,
Sick of " Eyes front " and " Attention,"
Came to London on his pension.
At the " Portland " as he stayed,
Firm the friendship that he made
With one William Richards, who
Put up at the " Portland " too.
Passed six years, then he was wrapped in
Love's embraces, vanquished captain !
" Yes," he cried, " I will ; no bar shall
Stop my wedding Edith Marshall."
But there was a bar, 'twas that
He was poorer than a rat ;
Indian pensions do not run
More than just enough for one.

Edith, too, had not a cent,

Who would pay the rates and rent?

Two more years, and Richards moved

(He perchance had sometime loved),

Promised them an income clear,

'Twas five hundred pounds a year

For his life; when he was dead,

Then ten thousand pounds instead.

This to Dashwood in a letter

Wrote he, deeming it was better

They should marry soon while he

Lived their happiness to see.

'Twas a modest sum, but marriage

May be blest without a carriage,

Forty pounds a month and more

Keep the wolf from near the door.

So they wed for worse or better,

On the faith of Richards' letter.

Scarcely was a quarter's payment

Due when mourning was their raiment.

Richards died. Alas! no cash would

Find its way to Captain Dashwood.

Dashwood's head began to swim—

Not a shilling left to him!

" Ha, I'll **have it** still," cried he ;

" Justice dwells in Chancery."

So the case was straightway taken

To the court of V.-C. Bacon.

Vainly Dashwood cash expended

The executors defended,

Claiming that what Richards wrote

Was not worth a five-pound note ;

First because the dead testator

Well, not wisely, loved the " cratur,"

More than that, had often been

In delirium tremens seen ;

Legal Lyrics

Secondly, because he signed

When he did not know his mind;

Third, because pollicitation

Is not good consideration.

Law, of justice independent,

Gave its judgment for defendant.

Poorer than he was at first,

That unhappy plaintiff cursed,

With a special satisfaction

Cursed the day he brought his action.

Would that he'd in India tarried!

Would that he had never married!

He, alas, is tied for life

Pauper to a pauper wife,

Scarce consoled that on his name

Equity reports shower fame,

Bearing down to endless ages

Dashwood's story on their pages.

EX PARTE JONES

(18 Chancery Division, 109)

OH for the wily infant who married the widow and made

Profit of coke and of breeze, and never a penny he paid !

Oh for the Corporation of Birmingham cheated and snared,

Taking orders for coke that the widow and infant prepared !

Oh for the Court of Appeal, and oh for Lords Justices three !

Oh for the Act that infants from contracts may shake themselves free !

Oh for the common law with its store of things old and new !

Birmingham coke is good and good Coke upon Littleton too.

Legal Lyrics

FINLAY *v.* CHIRNEY

(20 Queen's Bench Division, 494)

When love-sick man descends to folly

  And gets engaged, he must not stray,

The jury takes the part of Polly,

  And if he jilts her, he must pay.

The only way his fault to cover,

  From damages and costs to fly,

To leave his jilted lady-lover

  Without an action is—to die! *

POLLARD *v.* PHOTOGRAPHIC COMPANY

(40 Chancery Division, 345)

" Shall I take your photograph, my pretty maid ? "

" You may if you like, kind sir," she said.

* The decision was to the effect that in most cases an action for breach
of promise of marriage does not survive against the representatives of
the promiser.

71

" **Do you like** your photograph, my pretty **maid ? "**

" It is more than flattering, sir," she said.

" I'll publish your photograph, my pretty maid."

" Indeed but you won't, kind sir," **she said.**

" **As a Christmas** card, my pretty maid.**"**

" The very idea, kind sir ! " she said.

" **But what** if I've done it, my pretty maid ? **"**

" I'll **get an** injunction, sir," she said.

" The law is with you, my pretty maid,"

The learned judge of the Chancery said.

" **You** have proved the negative, my pretty maid,

A difficult thing in law," he said.

Legal Lyrics

THE MINNEAPOLIS CASE

(Tried in Minnesota in 1892)

KIND reader, tarry here, nor miss
The law of Minneapolis.
There was a carpenter called Brown,
A citizen of that great town,
Who stood his " inexpressive she "
A dollar's worth of comedy.
Was it a Gaiety burlesque,
Or labour of Norwegian desk?
Or did they spout in stagey tones
Morality by H. A. Jones?
Or tear romance to rags and set it
In heavy platitudes by Pettit?
I know not, and it matters not,
The subject I have clean forgot.

73

Sufficient that the pair did sit

In expectation in the pit,

An expectation not fulfilled,

'Twas otherwise by fortune willed.

Before this loving couple sat

In solitary state a hat—

A hat, I say, for in their wonder

They never noticed what was under,

The wearer must have been a "human,"

But might have been a man or woman.

'Twas like a mountain crowned with trees

Amid the pathless Pyrenees,

Or like a garden planned by Paxton,

Or colophon designed by Caxton,

So intricate the work ; and flowers

Were trained to climb its soaring towers,

Convolvulus and candytuft,

And 'mid them water-wagtails stuffed.

Such splendour never yet, I wis,

Had shone in Minneapolis.

But Brown was in a sore dilemma,

A dollar he had paid for Emma

To see a play, and not a hat;

A dollar, it was dear at that.

And Emma—disappointment racked her,

She never saw a single actor.

So Brown, with visage thunder-black,

Demanded both his dollars back.

The man who took the cash said, "Sonny,

Our rule is not to give back money.

But if you'll come another night,

Maybe you'll get a better sight."

So Brown went home and nursed his sorrow,

His writ he issued on the morrow.

A hundred dollars was his claim,

And the young lady claimed the same.

The case was argued, on revision

Of pleadings, this was the decision:

"The theatre's defence is bad,

Brown paid for what he never had,

He paid when in the pit he sat

To see a play and not a hat.

To bring defendants to their senses,

I find for plaintiffs with expenses."

Justitiæ columna sis,

Wise judge of Minneapolis!

Legal Lyrics

COMMONWEALTH *v.* MARZYNSKI

(21 New England Reports, 228 [Massachusetts, 1893])

[On a complaint for keeping open a tobacconist's shop on Sunday, contrary to the law of Massachusetts, it was held that the court will take judicial notice that tobacco and cigars are not drugs and medicines, and will exclude the testimony of a witness who offers evidence that they are.]

AGAINST the statutes of the Old Bay State

Marzynski on a Sunday stood behind

His counter, well content his gain to find

In pipes not pills, cigars not carbonate.

From breakfast till 'twas dusk at half-past eight

Tobacco cheered this hardened sinner's mind,

The price of it his pockets, disinclined

To add their dime to the collection plate.

The State Attorney claimed the penalty;

" Cigars are no cigars," said the defence,

" But drugs, and we have witnesses to prove it."

" Cigars to be cigars judicially

We notice, and reject the evidence."

So said the Court, and spat, and nought could

move it.

Translations

Translations

GREEK ANTHOLOGY

x. 48

WOE to the house whose mistress was a slave!

So say old saws, my own in aid I crave;

Woe to the court whose judge once spake for fees,

Though he were readier than Isocrates!

An advocate that pleaded once for pelf

Scarce on the bench forgets his former self.

Palladas.

XI. 75

THIS Olympicus of old

Had, Sebastus, I am told

Quite his share of upper gear,

Nose and chin and eye and ear.

All he lost, and by his fist—

He became a pugilist.

Loss of members with **it drew**

Loss of patrimony too.

When his birthright he would claim,

Into court his brother came

With a portrait, saying, " Thus

Looked the old Olympicus."

None could any likeness see,

Disinherited was he.

Lucillus.

XI. 141

A PIG, a goat, an ox I lost :

I want them back at any cost,

And so retained, O woful fate !

Menecles for my advocate.

But tell me, will you, what have these

In common with Othryades?

The heroes of Thermopylæ

Have nought to do with theft from me.

Against Eutychides I bring

My action for a trivial thing.

Let Xerxes rest a little space,

And leave the Spartans in their place.

For if you don't put all this by ,

I'll go into the streets and cry,

" The voice of Menecles is big,

But what about my stolen pig? "

Lucillus.

[This Epigram is probably an imitation of that of Martial, on p. 90.]

XI. 143

PLUTO rejected at his gate

The soul of Mark the advocate;

(6)   83

" No, Cerberus my dog," quoth he,

" Will make you pleasant company ;

But if within you needs must go,

Practise on poet Melito,

And **you shall** have, if he won't do,

Tityus and Ixion too.

You'll be to hell the sorest ill

Of all that hell contains, until

There come to us worse barbarisms

When Rufus speaks his solecisms."

Lucillus.

XI. 147

So soon hath Asiaticus

   The gift of eloquence achieved ?

It was in Thebes it happened thus,

   The story well may be believed.

Ammianus.

Legal Lyrics

THE statue of an advocate, as like as like can be.

And why? The statue cannot speak a word, no more

    could he.

Anon.

PAUL, dost thou wish to make thy boy

    An advocate like these his betters?

Then let him not his time employ

    To useless ends in learning letters.

Ammianus.

THE parties were as deaf as deaf could be,

The judge was far the deafest of the three.

Said plaintiff, " Sir, I ask for five months' rent."

Defendant, " Grinding corn all night I spent."

"Why," quoth the judge, "dispute? Your mother's
claim

Is good, and you must both support the dame."

Nicarchus.

XI. 350

REMEMBER justice and her yoke, and know

That 'gainst the wicked votes of "Guilty" go.

Thou trustest in thy cunning speech, thy power

Of speaking words that vary with the hour.

Hope what thou wilt, thy trifling tricks are vain,

Thou canst not make the path of law less plain.

Agathias.

XI. 376

ONCE to Diodorus came a client in a state of doubt,

And to that most learned counsel thus he set the
matter out:

"Alpha Beta found a slave-girl who had run away
from me:

To a slave of his he wed her, though she was my
 property,

Well he knew she was my chattel; she has had a
 child or two ;

Now I cannot tell for certain whose the children are,
 can you? "

Diodorus thought, consulted all authorities on " Slave,"

To his client turned his furrowed brows and slowly
 answer gave :

" 'Tis to you or to the other who, you say, has done
 you wrong,

That the children of the handmaid rightfully of course
 belong,

Your best plan will be the matter in the proper court
 to place,

So you'll get a good opinion whether you have any
 case."

Agathias.

PLAN, 193

"GOOD Hermes, only just one cabbage plant."

"**Stop**, stop, my thieving traveller, **you can't.**"

"**What,** grudge me one poor cabbage! is it so?"

"**Nay, I** don't grudge it, but the **law** says no.

The law says, **Keep** your itching palms, d'ye see,

From meddling with another's property."

"Well, this beats anything I ever saw!

Hermes against a thief invokes the law."

Philippus.

APPENDIX, 385

PUPILS seven of Aristides,

Tell me, how are ye?

Four of you **are** walls, beside is

Nought but **benches** three.

Legal Lyrics

Another Version

Seven pupils of the rhetor

Aristides, how are ye?

Seven! *Hoc et nihil præter*,

Four are walls and benches three.

Anon.

MARTIAL

In Caium

" LEND me sestertia, Caius, only twenty,

'Tis no great thing for you who roll in plenty."

He was an old companion, and his coffers

Were full enough to stand such friendly offers.

" Go, plead in court," said he; " 'tis pleadings pay us."

" I want your money, not your counsel, Caius."

Martial, ii. 30.

In Causidicum

'TIS said that some bold advocate
  Has dared to criticise my poem,
His name I have not learned, his fate
  Will be a warning when I know him.

Martial, v. 33.

In Postumum Causidicum

No claim for trespass do I bring,

Or homicide, or poisoning.

I claim that by my neighbour's theft
Of she-goats three I was bereft.
The judge of course wants evidence,
But you go wandering far from thence,
And with a mighty voice declaim
Of Mithridates and the shame

Of Cannæ, and the lies of old

That Punic politicians told.

And why should you pass Sylla by,

The Marii and Mucii?

When, Postumus, d'ye hope to reach

My stolen she-goats in your speech?

Martial, vi. 19.

In Cinnam

Is this advocacy, Cinna, this a type of lawyers' powers,

This immense oration, Cinna, some nine words in
some ten hours?

Waterclocks I grant you asked for, Cinna, yes, you
called for four;

There you stopped, such wealth of silence, Cinna,
ne'er was seen before.

Martial, viii. 7.

THE COURT OF REASON

A THOUSAND doubts and pleadings in a day
   Are filed in Empress Reason's court supreme
   By angry Love—his eyes with anger gleam.
   "Which of us twain hath been more faithful, say.
'Tis all through me that Cino can display
   The sail of fame on life's unhappy stream."
   "Thee," quoth I, "root of all my woe I deem,
   I found what gall beneath thy sweetness lay."
Then he: "Ah, traitorous and truant slave!
   Are these the thanks thou renderest, ingrate,
   For giving thee a maid without a peer?"
"Thy left," cried I, "slew what thy right hand gave."
   "Not so," said he.   The judge, "Your wrath abate.
   I must have time to give true judgment here."

Cino da Pistoia.

[Imitated by Petrarch in the conclusion of the Canzone, *Quell'
antico mio dolce empio signore.*]

TO ROME

TELL me, proud Rome, why dost these edicts read,

    These many laws by prince or people made,

    Or answers by the prudent duly weighed,

    When now thou canst the world no longer lead?

Thou readest, sad one, of each ancient deed

    Where thy unconquered sons their might displayed,

    Afric and Egypt at thy feet were laid,

    But slavery, not rule, is now thy meed.

What boots it that thou wast of old a queen,

    And over foreign nations heldest rein,

    If thou and all thy fame no more exist?

Forgive me, God, if all my days have been

    Devoted to man's laws, unjust and vain

    Unless Thy law within the heart be fixed.

Cino da Pistoia.

JUSTICE

AH! justice is a virtue bepraised and full of worth,

It castigates the sinner, and peoples **all the earth,**

And kings with care should guard it—instead **they**
now forget

The gem that is most precious in all the coronet.

Some think they may do justice by cruelty, I wist;

But 'tis an evil counsel, for justice must consist

In showing deeds of mercy, in knowledge of the truth,

And executing judgment it executes with ruth.

Pedro Lopez de Ayala.

THE POET AND THE ADVOCATE

GLORY and gain thus mixed distract the thought,

We owe to honour all, to fortune nought;

The poet, like the soldier, scorns for **pay**

Peruvian gold, but seeks the wreath **of bay.**

Legal Lyrics

How is the advocate the poet's peer?
The poet's glory is complete and clear ;
He far outlives the advocate's renown,
Patru is e'en by Scarron's name weighed down.
The bar of Greece and Rome you point me out,
A bar that trained great men, I do not doubt,
For then chicane with language void of sense
Had not deformed the law and eloquence.
Purge the tribune of all this monstrous growth,
I mount it, and my soul will sink, though loth,
Will yield to fortune and will speak in prose.
But since reform in this so slowly grows,
Leave me my tastes, for I aspire to be
By verse ennobled to posterity,
To hold first place in arts above the law,
More grave and noble than it ever saw.
Fraud in this age of ours unpunished can
Tread down the equity so dear to man.

Can you for spirits just and generous find

A fairer cause to plead before mankind?

Mother or stepmother let Fortune be,

The theatre and not the bar for me;

For client virtue, truth for counsel's wage,

For judge the present and the coming age.

Piron, La Métromanie, Act iii. Sc. 7.

MORRISON AND GIBB, PRINTERS, EDINBURGH.